HIP-HOP
MOGULS

An Unauthorized Biography

Jay-Z
Hip-Hop Mogul

John Albert Torres

Speeding Star
Keep Boys Reading!

Library of Congress Cataloging-in-Publication Data

Torres, John Albert.
    Jay-Z : hip-hop mogul / John Albert Torres.
        pages cm. — (Hip-hop moguls)
    Includes bibliographical references and index.
    Summary: "In this biography of Hip-Hop mogul Jay-Z, read everything about him from his rough
childhood in Brooklyn to his rise to fame as a rapper and entrepreneur"-- Provided by publisher.
    ISBN 978-1-62285-191-1
    1. Jay-Z, 1969—Juvenile literature. 2. Rap musicians—United States—Biography—Juvenile
literature. I. Title.
    ML3930.J38T67 2014
    782.421649092—dc23
    [B]   2013048804

Future Editions:
Paperback ISBN: 978-1-62285-192-8   EPUB ISBN: 978-1-62285-193-5
Single-User PDF ISBN: 978-1-62285-194-2   Multi-User PDF: 978-1-62285-195-9

Printed in the United States of America
052014 Lake Book Manufacturing, Inc., Melrose Park, IL
10 9 8 7 6 5 4 3 2 1

To Our Readers: This book has not been authorized by Jay-Z or his agents.

We have done our best to make sure all Internet addresses in this book were active and appropriate when
we went to press. However, the author and the Publisher have no control over, and assume no liability for,
the material available on those Internet sites or on other Web sites they may link to. Any comments or sug-
gestions can be sent by e-mail to comments@speedingstar.com or to the address below:

Speeding Star
Box 398, 40 Industrial Road
Berkeley Heights, NJ 07922
USA
www.speedingstar.com

♻ Enslow Publishers, Inc., is committed to printing our books on recycled paper. The paper in every book
contains 10% to 30% post-consumer waste (PCW). The cover board on the outside of each book contains
100% PCW. Our goal is to do our part to help young people and the environment too!

Illustration Credits: ©AP Images/Alan Diaz, p. 25; ©AP Images/Andy Kropa, pp. 9, 35; ©AP Images/
Brad Barket, p. 18; ©AP Images/Charles Sykes, p. 13; ©AP Images/Chris Carlson, p. 28; ©AP Images/
Chris Pizzello, p. 34; ©AP Images/Evan Agostini, p. 21; ©AP Images/Gary He, p. 4; ©AP Images/Henny
Ray Abrams, p. 39; ©AP Images/Jack Plunkett, p. 10; ©AP Images/Jason DeCrow, p. 26; ©AP Images/
Julie Jacobson, p. 8; ©AP Images/Kathy Willens, pp. 20, 40; ©AP Images/Matt Sayles, pp. 6, 15, 27, 32;
©AP Images/Rich Schultz, p. 33; ©AP Images/Roc Nation Sports, p. 42.

Cover Illustration: ©AP Images/Gary He

Contents

It's rare that someone is able to go out on top. Athletes, movie stars, singers, and celebrities all tend to stick around past their prime. It's not often that someone can retire right after accomplishing greatness. In baseball, Ted Williams blasted a home run in his very last at-bat. Yankees pitcher Mariano Rivera had a great season in 2013, even though he had announced it would be his last.

Music is no different. Jay-Z was already considered by many people to be the greatest rapper of all-time when

Chapter 1

Worst Retirement

Jay-Z

Jay-Z holds up his signature hand symbol, which is known as the dynasty sign. It represents Roc-A-Fella, his record label, that he sold to Def Jam Recordings around the time he "retired."

he announced in 2003 that his next studio album, his eighth, would be his very last. He would be retiring from recording any more solo albums and giving concerts.

He was only thirty-three, but Jay-Z felt that he had reached the highest level he could as a performer.

Disappointed fans waited anxiously for the record to be released. Would it be any good? Was Jay-Z burnt out? Had we already seen his best?

The Black Album was a home run. If Jay-Z was going to retire, then he was going out on top. The album was released on November 14, 2003 and roared up the music charts to the number one spot in its first week, selling 463,000 copies. It wasn't only the fans who thought the album was great. The critics also heralded the recording as the rapper's best ever.

Music critic Steve Jones of the *USA Today* newspaper gave the record the highest ranking—four out of four stars—and said Jay-Z was working on a level all his own. *RapReviews.com* said it was not a good record but a great record!

One of the keys to the record was that Jay-Z was able to use his star power and pull in a lot of high-powered producers and other artists to join him on the record. Some of the guest stars included Kanye West, The Neptunes, Timbaland, Eminem, and Just Blaze.

Three songs from *The Black Album* became hit singles. They were: "Change Clothes," "Dirt Off Your Shoulder," and "99 Problems." The record was just another example of what made Jay-Z the most talented

and most popular rapper on the planet—his ability to rap lyrics effortlessly with just about any type of music.

Like Ted Williams and Mariano Rivera, Jay-Z would be going out on top.

No retirement is complete without a party and so that's just what Jay-Z planned, the ultimate retirement party concert. He called it the Fade to Black concert,

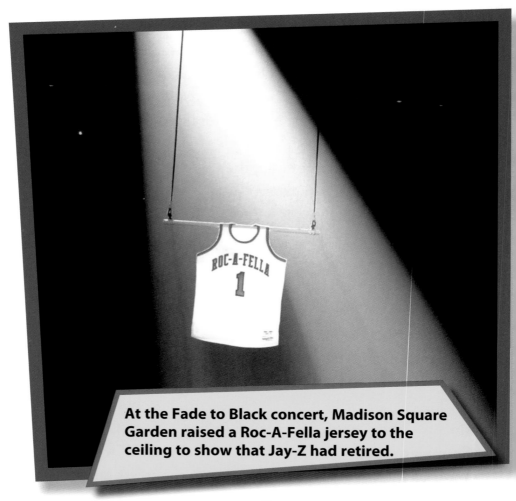

At the Fade to Black concert, Madison Square Garden raised a Roc-A-Fella jersey to the ceiling to show that Jay-Z had retired.

Another concert that Jay-Z put together at Madison Square Garden was the Answer the Call concert in 2009. All proceeds raised at the show were given to the New York Police & Fire Widows' and Children's Benefit Fund.

which would be filmed and produced into a movie called *Fade to Black*.

The retirement party became a who's who of the rap and R&B music industry. Several high-profile acts joined Jay-Z onstage at New York's Madison Square Garden and took part in the fun. They included acts and performers such as: The Roots, Beyoncé, R. Kelly, Mary J. Blige, and Foxy Brown among others.

9

All the proceeds from the concert went to charity. This was not unusual for the man who has never forgotten his roots, the poverty he had to overcome, and the struggles he faced in making it to the top of the music industry.

Jay-Z continued working even though he was "retired." He produced albums for other recording artists including rock group Linkin Park and Fort Minor. He also became the president of Def Jam Records. And he became a part-owner of the NBA basketball team the New Jersey Nets, now known as the Brooklyn Nets.

Jay-Z quickly reclaimed his spot on top of the hip-hop world after ending his retirement.

10

But Jay-Z missed the limelight, missed recording his own music, and missed going out on the road. It wasn't long before he realized that retiring was a big mistake. Making millions of music fans across the world happy, Jay-Z announced that he was un-retiring.

"It was the worst retirement in history," he told *Entertainment Weekly* magazine in 2006. He explained that he made the decision to resume his career after spending some time alone in his music studio. "Something, when you love it, is always tugging at you and itching and I was putting it off and putting it off. I started fumbling around to see if it felt good."

It must have felt good, because before long Jay-Z found himself back in front of a microphone doing what he does best. Pretty soon, the album *Kingdom Come* was released and the world's most famous rapper found himself in a familiar place—on top of the music charts.

He made fans two promises at that time. First, he would keep making music and rapping until he no longer had anything to say. Second, he would never again announce that he was retiring.

He was back on top. It was a far cry from his humble beginnings, growing up in one of Brooklyn's worst drug-infested neighborhoods and the violence that he had become used to. It was also a far cry from the biggest mistake he ever made: selling drugs as a youngster.

Shawn Corey Carter was born on December 4, 1969. Carter, who goes by the stage name Jay-Z, was born and raised in Brooklyn, N.Y. Brooklyn is one of the five boroughs that make up the city of New York.

While there are some very nice parts of Brooklyn, Jay-Z grew up in a housing project called the Marcy Houses located in the gritty and tough Bedford-Stuyvesant neighborhood. Housing projects are public housing for families with very low incomes.

Chapter 2

Growing Up

Things were made even more difficult when his father, Adnes Reeves, left the family when Jay-Z was still a boy. He was only eleven years old. His mother, Gloria Carter, was forced to provide for and raise Jay-Z—the youngest of her four children—and his three siblings by herself. He has two older sisters—Michelle and Andrea, and one older brother, Eric.

"He was the last of my four children," Gloria Carter would later say. "He was the only one who didn't give me

Jay-Z's story gives hope to people growing up in poverty, because he has risen to the absolute top of the world. This is him at the grand re-opening of his club, the 40/40 Club, in New York City.

any pain when I gave birth to him, and that's how I knew he was a special child."

She was only partly right. While Jay-Z would grow up to be one of the most beloved rappers of all time, he gave her plenty of trouble and plenty to worry about when he was a youngster.

Something happened when Jay-Z was only twelve years old that would haunt him for the rest of his life. His older brother, Eric—who was sixteen years old —had become a drug addict. Like most drug addicts, Eric started stealing in order to have enough money to buy his drugs. One afternoon, Jay-Z caught his brother stealing his jewelry and reacted with rage.

Being raised with so much violence around him, Jay-Z did what seemed normal to him at the time. He went to a friend's house and got a gun. Guns were everywhere back then and easy to get. He shot his brother with it, sending a bullet straight through his shoulder. The police came, and Eric was taken to the hospital. The wound was not life-threatening.

"I thought my life was over. I thought I'd go to jail forever…it was terrible. I was a boy, a child. I was terrified," he told a London newspaper a few years ago.

Luckily, for the young boy, his brother never blamed him. In fact, he insisted that police not arrest his younger brother and told them he did not want to press any charges. When Jay-Z and his family went to see Eric in the hospital, it was Eric who apologized.

He told his family he was sorry for being on drugs and for doing the things he had done.

Jay-Z rarely talks about that part of his life, but does express his feelings about it in a song he wrote called "You Must Love Me."

The truth is that drugs were a very big part of Jay-Z's childhood. The Marcy Houses were infested with drugs.

After what happened with his brother, Jay-Z turned his life around. Now he often finds himself on the receiving end of many top awards, like these three Grammy awards he won in 2013.

It was the 1980s and crack cocaine was the drug of choice. It was cheap to buy and very addicting. In interviews, Jay-Z said he could smell drug addicts smoking crack in the hallways of the apartment building where he lived. He said he could smell the drug the minute he opened the door.

It wasn't a good situation to grow up in. With no father around, Jay-Z's mother, Gloria, did her best to make sure her son stayed out of trouble. But that became nearly impossible because she had to work. Maybe things would have been different if his father had stayed around and provided a male role model. Jay-Z had a lot of freedom and, like his brother Eric, he started making the wrong choices and bad mistakes.

For kids growing up in that type of environment, many times the only male role models they have are the drug dealers in their fancy cars with wads of cash.

During the crack cocaine epidemic, young boys in the projects either became drug addicts or they started selling the drug on street corners. The latter was the road Jay-Z would take. It was a road of danger and regret and one that would see him shot at three different times.

"(The drugs were rough) especially in that neighborhood. It was a plague in that neighborhood," he said. "It was just everywhere, everywhere you look."

Jay-Z was only still a kid when he decided the best way to support himself and not become a drug addict would be to start selling it.

Jay-Z says that his mother gave him a long leash growing up. He was given a lot of freedom to do what he wanted. He had just become a teenager when he made the decision to sell drugs.

He was on the corner every day selling crack cocaine to the drug addicts. He was making more money than he ever thought he would. But it was at this time that Jay-Z began to rap lyrics inside his head. He was known on the streets as Jazzy,

Chapter 3

From Drugs to Music

a nickname he carried since he was a child. He admits to being kind of a lost soul.

"I had no aspirations, no plans, no goals, no back-up goals," he told the television show *60 Minutes*.

What he did have was a knack for coming up with lyrical rhymes, the cornerstone of rap music. He would sometimes stay up late in the kitchen of the small apartment he grew up in and would bang out rhythms

Jay-Z went from making beats and rhythms in the kitchen of his apartment to performing at the largest venues, such as the Victoria's Secret Fashion Show with his buddy Kanye West.

on the kitchen table. But it got to the point that he was keeping his family awake at night.

So, his mother Gloria bought her son a boom box radio for his birthday. Able to listen to rap music regularly now and being able to study the rhythms and patterns, Jay-Z started turning his attention from selling drugs to making music.

"I used to get ideas and I used to be running around, I used to be outside," he told *60 Minutes.* "I wasn't nowhere where I could write. Sometimes I used to run in the store, write 'em on a paper bag, put it in my pocket. But you only can put so many paper bags in your pocket, you know—and so I had to start memorizing."

That ability to memorize his lyrics helped Jay-Z win several rapping contests as a teenager. It carries through to today, as he still does not write down his lyrics.

While he attended three high schools, he never was able to get his diploma. Jay-Z is most notably remembered for his time at Brooklyn's George Westinghouse Career and Technical Education High School. Incredibly, he attended school at the same time as two other famous rappers—Busta Rhymes and The Notorious B.I.G.

It was because he was so good at memorizing lyrics and coming up with rhymes on the spot that he was reportedly able to defeat future stars like Busta Rhymes, DMX, and Bizzy Bone during rap battles.

Jay-Z continued selling drugs until something terrible happened that made him question what he was doing. Drugs are a very violent—and of course illegal—business.

It is not uncommon for those involved in drugs to wind up dead or in prison. Jay-Z would be no different.

He was shot at three times, all from a very close distance, but fortunately he was never hit. He would later say that it was as if an angel was looking out for him. That is when he would stop selling drugs and start to focus on his music.

Jay-Z was inspired and influenced a bit by the music he used to hear his mother listening to. That's why he credits great soul and R&B recording artists such as Marvin Gaye and Donny Hathaway as being among his main influences.

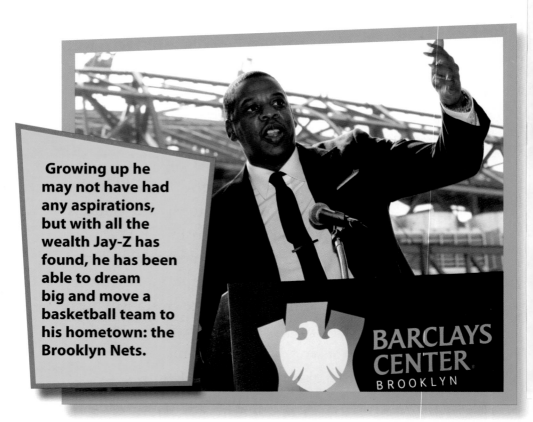

Growing up he may not have had any aspirations, but with all the wealth Jay-Z has found, he has been able to dream big and move a basketball team to his hometown: the Brooklyn Nets.

This is a shot of Jay-Z's longtime friend and cofounder of Roc-A-Fella Records, Damon Dash.

It was during this time that he met and became friends with a young rapper by the name of Jonathan Burks, who rapped under the name Jaz-O. Burks recorded a song called "The Originators" Some of Jay-Z's lyrics are featured on the record, and that became his first real taste of the music industry. Burks became a mentor of sorts to Jay-Z, showing him the ropes of the music business. The two performed a song on *Yo! MTV Raps*, a music program on television.

He continued rapping and recording songs and tried to get a recording deal, but no one would sign him. That didn't stop him. He started recording songs with his friend, Damon Dash, and making CDs. He would drive around neighborhoods with the music blasting from his car's stereo and out through the open windows. He would ask people if they liked what they heard and then he would offer to sell them copies of his CD.

It was about this time that Jay-Z stopped being known as "Jazzy" and took on the name Jay-Z. It was partly a play on his childhood nickname, partly to honor Jaz-O, and it was partly to honor his neighborhood. The J/Z train stop is located in the neighborhood he grew up in, the Marcy Houses.

Even with lots of people buying and enjoying his music, Jay-Z could not find a record label that would sign him and record his songs. But that was never going to stop him. He kept writing and recording and continued selling CDs out of his car.

And when Jay-Z realized that he was unlikely to be signed, he and Dash decided to do the very next best thing: they started their own record company.

Since no one would sign him to a record label, Jay-Z, his friend Damon Dash, and Kareem Burke started their own independent record label. They named it Roc-A-Fella Records in 1995 and rented a small, shabby office in Brooklyn for their company. They made a deal with a separate company to distribute the records they produced.

For Jay-Z it was time to get into the studio and start to record his music. The result was his debut album called *Reasonable Doubt*.

Chapter 4

Rise to Stardom

The soon-to-be-superstar had some help. Appearing on the record was The Notorious B.I.G., who was one of the biggest names in hip-hop at the time. He also had help from some popular rap record producers like Super DJ Clark Kent and DJ Premier.

The album was an immediate hit for this new rapper by the name of Jay-Z. It reached No. 23 on the record charts. Years later, *Rolling Stone* magazine would rank it as one of the greatest albums of all time. It helped a lot that Jay-Z was touring with Big Daddy Kane and also appearing on records of other rap artists at this time as well. It helped to get his name out there and make him recognizable.

Four singles were released from the record and all did very well. *Reasonable Doubt* is considered by many to be Jay-Z's best album. The artist himself has called it his most "honest" work and the most lyrical songs he has ever written.

But this was only the beginning for the poor kid from the Brooklyn housing projects. In fact, it would be the lowest charting album he would ever do.

The following year, Jay-Z turned to famous rapper and record producer Sean "Puffy" Combs (aka Puff Daddy, P. Diddy) to produce and record and release his second album, *In My Lifetime, Vol. 1*. This recording had a much different feel than his first album. It was more polished and professional, and the sound was better. While it did well on the charts, many fans liked the gritty, edgier, rough sound of *Reasonable Doubt*.

Despite the different sound, the album was a huge success and actually did better than *Reasonable Doubt* on the charts. Jay-Z would later say that the album was very difficult to do. He was dealing with some personal issues at the time, including the shooting death of one of his oldest and closest friends, Christopher Wallace — the rapper known as The Notorious B.I.G.

Some people believed that B.I.G. had been killed in retaliation for the shooting death of West Coast rapper

Jay-Z and Sean "Diddy" Combs have teamed up on other ventures since Combs help produce Jay-Z's second major studio album. This includes a campaign rally to support Barack Obama when he was running for president.

Whether or not they ever had any personal issues, Jay-Z and Snoop Dogg were involved in the ongoing East Coast vs. West Coast rivalry that resulted in the deaths of Tupac Shakur and The Notorious B.I.G

Tupac Shakur. There had been a rivalry between the two stars and a lot of bad feelings between the two coasts and their different styles of rap music.

Jay-Z channeled his grief and sorrow into the music. Fans loved it, and he was now very well-known and on his way to becoming a star.

The new rising star did not want to let any time lapse between his records. So he continued appearing on other rapper's songs, and he also got right back in the studio to record his third album in three years.

In 1998, he released the instant classic *Vol. 2… Hard Knock Life*. The song "Hard Knock Life (Ghetto Anthem)" was a smash hit song, becoming popular almost immediately after the album was released.

The song appealed to his normal rap audience and crossed over into the mainstream music fans. The reason? He used the background music and lyrics from a song called "Hard Knock Life" from the famous musical

Jamie Foxx, a well-known actor and fellow musician presents Jay-Z with the Grammy for Best Rap/Sung Collaboration at the 2014 Grammy Awards.

and children's story *Annie* that was based on the classic comic book strip "Little Orphan Annie."

In the music industry, the highest honor any artist can win is the trophy called a Grammy. Many great artists go their entire careers never winning the coveted Grammy. It's very special to win one and it's even special to get nominated for one.

Jay-Z and Beyoncé began dating after teaming up on a few songs. The couple was married on April 4, 2008.

Jay-Z's third album not only got nominated, but it actually won the prestigious award for the Best Rap Album.

He was making millions of dollars and gaining millions of fans, but now Jay-Z had also earned the respect of the music industry. His next album also became a huge hit. It was called *Vol. 3… Life and Times of S. Carter.* He had become so popular that the following year he appeared on a song with pop superstar Mariah Carey, who was on top of the music industry at this point.

It was the same type of teaming up with a pop star that would eventually lead to marriage between Jay-Z and Beyoncé Knowles in 2008.

Meanwhile, in the late 1990s, Jay-Z continued churning out one great album and one hit record after another. His rapping style has been admired and copied by many. In a book called *How to Rap,* some fellow rappers say what sets Jay-Z apart is the smooth flow of the words as they come out of his mouth. They said it didn't matter if he was rapping a fast song or a slow one, his flow always remained smooth. He had come a long way from the kid forced to sell drugs on the street corner.

Jay-Z would regularly appear on pop star's tracks and records. The reason this was done was to appeal to a wider audience. Rap music fans would like the song because Jay-Z was on it, and the pop star's fans would like it because of the pop star.

In 2002, he teamed up with singer Beyoncé Knowles, known simply as Beyoncé. She was the lead singer and a major part of the all-girl group known as Destiny's Child. But now she was branching out on her own and trying to establish herself as a true solo recording artist. She was

Chapter 5

Romance

a beautiful artist with a powerful voice. They recorded the song "'03 Bonnie & Clyde," for Jay-Z's album that became a huge hit song and music video. They also did another song for her album called "Crazy in Love."

America loved it and loved the new power couple. "Crazy in Love" became the No. 1 song in the country and the message rang true. The two musical superstars hit it off, began dating, and soon fell in love.

Meanwhile, while he was touring in France in 2003, the rapper decided it might be time to call it quits. Maybe he was tired from the grind of performing all the time. Maybe he wanted to spend more time with Beyoncé. Maybe he really did just want to be a record producer. Or maybe he just didn't want to end up like his friend, "Biggie Smalls," The Notorious B.I.G.

Whatever the reason, Jay-Z said he was retiring and *The Black Album*, his eighth studio album, would be his last. The album was terrific, as was his retirement party and concert called the "Fade to Black" concert. He then took over as president of Def Jam Records.

Of course, we know that his retirement did not last long. Music fans are thankful that he soon re-emerged to make hit albums and singles.

In 2006, he recorded *Kingdom Come* and followed that up a year later with *American Gangster*. *American Gangster* did not sell as well as some of his others, but it was a very personal recording for Jay-Z. In it, he tells the story of growing up on drug-infested streets and committing illegal acts to make money before becoming a musical performer. He mentions things in his songs that he never really spoke about in public.

That year he teamed up on another Beyoncé album that produced another hit record for the woman who would soon be his wife.

Jay-Z and Beyoncé have not only maintained a strong relationship, but they also continue to put out new songs together. One of these hit songs is "Drunk in Love."

While technically still retired, Jay-Z performed with Kanye West at the Summer Jam 2005 concert.

Around this time, Jay-Z started getting involved in many other business ventures. He started a clothing line called Rocawear that appealed to the hip-hop crowd. He also invested money in a chain of hotels and bought a minority share of an English soccer team! Because he was so busy with his new ventures, and also back to recording music full time, Jay-Z stepped down as president of Def Jam Records.

On April 4, 2008, Jay-Z and Beyoncé got married during a small ceremony. The couple is very private about their relationship and rarely speak about it in

public. Jay-Z, especially, refuses to speak about his relationship with Beyoncé when he grants interviews.

"What Jay and I have is real. It's not about interviews or getting the right photo op," Beyoncé told a magazine six months after the wedding. "It's real." The new bride went on to say that she wasn't interested in a big wedding and all the drama that comes with it. She has seen too many celebrity marriages fall apart. She felt that sometimes the gossip and the limelight in the

Jay-Z and Chris Martin of Coldplay share a laugh at the 2009 Grammy Awards.

Jay-Z has a large list of charities and foundations that he gives to. One such organization is LeBron James's Family Foundation. Jay-Z is shown here with tennis star Serena Williams (middle) and LeBron James (right).

newspapers and magazines can hurt a couple and cause them to split up.

Some of the celebrities who shared the couple's day included actress Gwyneth Paltrow and members of Beyoncé's former band, Destiny's Child. The party was held under a tent on the roof of a New York City building where the couple lives. It was a small but extravagant affair.

As part of their vows of love to each other, the couple had the Roman numeral "IV" tattooed on their ring fingers. The number four has special meaning for the couple as they each have a birthday on the fourth and they were married on the fourth.

Meanwhile, both music stars' careers continued to rise. For example, Jay-Z found an entirely new audience when he recorded a version of the song "Lost" with the world-famous rock band Coldplay. The lead singer of Coldplay, Chris Martin was Paltrow's husband at the time. Paltrow and Martin have always been close friends with Beyoncé and Jay-Z.

Over the next few years Jay-Z focused mainly on collaborative projects with other artists.

He also decided to publish a book detailing his childhood and life in a memoir called *Decoded*. The book contained lyrics to thirty-six Jay-Z songs and included what the lyrics meant. Over the next few years, Jay-Z would diversify even more and make the decision to give back to those less fortunate.

Jay-Z grew up in a public housing project. He knows what it's like to be poor and have to worry about your next meal. That's what makes it so easy for him to give back to the community, and to get involved with trying to make the world a better place. But he's the kind of artist who didn't just want to give money to some charity, he really wanted to make sure he was making a difference.

It all started when Jay-Z noticed the kind of charitable work that the rock star Bono — of the group U2 — was doing

Chapter 6

Giving Back

in Africa. Bono has long been involved in trying to help the poor and sick of Africa. He has started several charities to help the continent deal with AIDS and Malaria, two diseases that have killed millions of people in Africa. Jay-Z took a trip over there and noticed that many of the people's problems stem from not having enough clean water.

In the United States, we take clean water for granted. We know that we just have to turn on the faucet and we will have clean water. That is not the case in many parts of the world, where people have to rely on wells to get their daily water.

Jay-Z decided to meet with leaders of the United Nations to see what he could do. He decided to use his world tour to raise awareness and money for clean water in Africa. He produced a documentary about his efforts to help Africa called *Diary of Jay-Z: Water for Life*. His work was so impressive that a few years later the United Nations made him the spokesman for the global water shortage.

"In the beginning, when I was going out on a world tour, I was going out to play music," he told *Billboard* magazine. "But I said to myself, I can't go to these places I've been and not go out and see the people that have been touched by my music for over ten years. I'm going to help and see what I can do in these areas. Every fifteen seconds a child dies from not having clean water. That's just staggering numbers and I figured that if the information was out and young people knew that these problems exist that they'd get involved."

But that wasn't the only charity that Jay-Z has gotten involved in. After Hurricane Katrina flooded the city of New Orleans, the popular rap star donated $1 million to the American Red Cross to help lead relief efforts.

He has also donated money and clothing to the Spring Hill Campaign for Adolescent and University Student Empowerment (CAUSE) and raised money for PlayPumps International.

Jay-Z (shown here with Kofi Annan) has used his fame and fortune to help benefit many good causes. One example is his work with the United Nations to raise worldwide awareness about the need for cleaner water.

When Jay-Z became a minority owner of the New Jersey Nets, he was one of the biggest voices behind getting the team to relocate to his native Brooklyn.

In addition to the charity work and rap music, Jay-Z continues to branch out into other businesses. Besides the clothing lines and hotels, Jay-Z also got involved in his favorite sport—basketball.

When the Brooklyn-born rapper heard that the New Jersey Nets basketball team was being sold, he thought it would be cool to own a small part of the team. Then he really got involved when he heard the people looking to buy the team were looking to move the team from New Jersey to Brooklyn.

Even though he only owned less than one percent of the team, Jay-Z became the face of the Brooklyn Nets as they worked hard to transform a terrible basketball team into a playoff powerhouse. He also became a partner for the new arena that the Nets would be playing in—the Barclays Center.

His involvement with the team would eventually open another door for Jay-Z to go through, but it would mean that he would have to sell his share of the team. He noticed that many athletes were unhappy with the agents that were representing them. Some athletes even told Jay-Z that they wished he was a sports agent since he was so good at business and was a sports fan at the same time.

He thought about it long and hard and decided to try his hand at becoming a sports agent. He started Roc Nation Sports Management and became an agent for some famous baseball, football, and basketball players. Some of the well-known athletes that signed with him

right away included All-Star second baseman Robinson Cano, All-Star pitcher C.C. Sabathia, NBA superstar Kevin Durant, and NFL quarterback Geno Smith. The agent is the person who tries to get the best deal for their player from the teams they play for. They can also serve as an advisor, mentor, and help the athlete with business opportunities away from sports, including doing commercials on television. However, Jay-Z would not

One of Jay-Z's superstar clients that signed on with Roc Nation Sports is New York Yankees All-Star pitcher C.C. Sabathia (left).

have been able to represent basketball players if he was still an owner of the Nets.

In 2013, he sold his share of the Brooklyn Nets to the team's new head coach, Jason Kidd, who once played for the Nets when they played in New Jersey. But Jay-Z remains close with the team and is a huge fan. He is often seen cheering for the team in his usual courtside seat.

He was also forced to sell his share as an owner of the Barclays Center, and according to *Forbes* magazine, he pocketed $1.5 million because the center has been doing so well with attracting sporting events and concerts.

"Our newest endeavor is committed to building the brands of professional athletes as we have done for some of today's top music artists," Jay-Z wrote. "For Roc Nation Sports to function at its full potential, NBA rules stipulate that I relinquish my ownership in the Brooklyn Nets."

It's amazing to think that Jay-Z has time for anything else. But something happened in 2012 that he definitely makes time for—the birth of his daughter Blue Ivy. After the rough childhood he experienced and the absence of a father figure, he vowed to work hard at being the best father he could be. One of the first things he did for his daughter was to write and record a song for her called "Glory."

If you listen carefully at the end of the song you can hear his daughter crying in the background. Because her cries can be heard, she had to be credited as a singer on the record. She was only two days old, so this made her

the youngest singer ever to be on a record that made the charts.

We already know how much Jay-Z loves basketball, but we also know he loves to play video games. He said it was a thrill to work on the video game *NBA 2K13*. He was asked to help work on the "feel" of the game to make it more realistic and gritty. And, of course, the makers of the game asked him to help out with the music.

It's clear that Jay-Z will never be satisfied with his life. He will always strive to do more, to be better, and to try new things. Jay-Z always does the unpredictable. But one thing is certain, Jay-Z will always be known as one of the best rappers of all-time.

Discography

Reasonable Doubt, 1996

In My Lifetime, Vol. 1, 1997

Vol. 2… Hard Knock Life, 1998

Vol. 3… Life and Times of S. Carter, 1999

The Dynasty: Roc La Familia 2000, 2000

The Blueprint, 2001

The Blueprint²: The Gift & the Curse, 2002
(Re-released as *The Blueprint 2.1* in 2003)

The Black Album, 2003

Kingdom Come, 2006

American Gangster, 2007

The Blueprint 3, 2009

Magna Carta… Holy Grail, 2013

Internet Addresses

OFFICIAL JAY-Z FAN PAGE
https://www.facebook.com/JayZ
OFFICIAL TWITTER PAGE
https://twitter.com/S_C_

Selected Honors and Awards

1999	Best Rap Album, Grammy Awards
2004	Best Rap/Sung Collaboration (with Beyoncé), Grammy Awards
	Best R&B Song (with Beyoncé, Rich Harrison, and Eugene Record), Grammy Awards
2005	Best Rap Solo Performance, Grammy Awards
2006	Hip-Hop Hustler Award, BET Hip-Hop Awards
	Best Rap/Sung Collaboration (with Linkin Park), Grammy Awards
2008	Best Rap/Sung Collaboration (with Rihanna), Grammy Awards
2009	Best Live Performer, BET Hip-Hop Awards
	Hustler of the Year, BET Hip-Hop Awards
	Lyricist of the Year, BET Hip-Hop Awards
	MVP of the Year, BET Hip-Hop Awards
	Best Rap Performance by a Duo or Group (with T.I., Kanye West, and Lil Wayne), Grammy Awards
2010	Best Hip-Hop Video (with Alicia Keys), BET Hip-Hop Awards
	Best Live Performance, BET Hip-Hop Awards
	CD of the Year, BET Hip-Hop Awards
	Perfect Combo Award (with Alicia Keys), BET Hip-Hop Awards

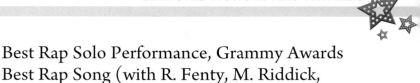

Best Rap Solo Performance, Grammy Awards

Best Rap Song (with R. Fenty, M. Riddick, Kanye West, and E. Wilson), Grammy Awards

Best Rap/Sung Collaboration (with Rihanna and Kanye West), Grammy Awards

2011   Hustler of the Year, BET Hip-Hop Awards

Best Rap Performance by a Duo or Group (with Swizz Beatz), Grammy Awards

Best Rap Song (with Angela Hunte, Burt Keyes, Alicia Keys, Jane't Sewell-Ulepic, Alexander Shuckburgh), Grammy Awards

Best Rap/Sung Collaboration (with Alicia Keys), Grammy Awards

2012   CD of the Year (with Kanye West), BET Hip-Hop Awards

Best Rap Song (with Kanye West), Grammy Awards

2013   Best Live Performer, BET Hip-Hop Awards

Hustler of the Year, BET Hip-Hop Awards

Rap Performance (with Kanye West), Grammy Awards

Rap Song (with Kanye West), Grammy Awards

Rap/Sung Collaboration (with Kanye West, Frank Ocean, and The Dream), Grammy Awards

2014   Best Music Video (with Justin Timberlake), Grammy Awards

Best Rap/Sung Collaboration (with Justin Timberlake), Grammy Awards

Index